MOON WARRIOR'S DREAM

JESUS VELAZQUEZ

DEDICATION

To my wife Elaine and my children Jayson, Jesseline and Jessica . . .

JESUS VELAZQUEZ

The dream is the same almost every night; it never changes. I'm running towards my enemy, full of anger and fear. I tackle him and we engage in hand to hand combat but he has a sharp object in one hand and a tomahawk in the other. I don't know where we are, all I know is we are wrestling; or should I say I'm trying to stay alive. He is much bigger and stronger than I am. As we roll on the ground, I end up on my back and he is over me, one hand on my throat the other about to scalp me. I'm frozen I don't move; I can't move . . . then I wake up . . . sweaty and scared. I say to myself, we are not warriors; we are peaceful people. I can't go back to sleep, so I go to the most peaceful place I know—under the willow tree up on the ridge overlooking the villages.

Every year when the air is cooler and the leaves begin to change color, we have what we call the gathering. People from many villages come to an open plain, not far from my village, to trade in food, furs, traps and trinkets, whatever is needed, and especially to get ready for the white season. I enjoy going every year, seeing my friends and the different tribes. One tribe I do not wish to see, however, is the tribe that makes their home near the great water. These people always ask for more than their goods are worth. Mother deals with them calmly. She says they have many hardships every white season so she understands them to some degree. The main reason I enjoy going and am probably the only boy who loves going to the gathering is because I enjoy seeing my friend Yanyan.

Yanyan is different. Like me, she enjoys the sounds of the forest: the animals, plants, and trees. We play many games together like pitching pebbles (that's a game where we throw pebbles across the stream to see who gets the closest to the other side without touching the riverbank.) When we are together, the hours feel like minutes. Our mothers always end up looking for us, worried and scared knowing that sometimes we'll keep walking and talking, going deeper and deeper into the forest to the point of sometimes getting lost.

Back home, Namoo is my best friend, almost like a brother. He is an adventurer and is always getting into trouble with his parents for wandering into the forest with me . . . he never says no . . . always up for an adventure. As I go to my favorite spot under the willow tree on the ridge overlooking the villages, I notice something each day moving northeast. It is a small camp . . . maybe a herd of animals, I'm not quite sure, but I know it's moving northeast towards Yanyan's village. However, I can't tell anyone because I'm not supposed to be here. The village elders have already complained to my mom several times this month.

I'm always the first one done with my chores, so that I can go to the forest and just enjoy my surroundings. As I head back to my village, I notice a small gathering; it does not look good. I see several men from Yanyan's village, hurt, and bloodied as if they were in combat or some animal had attacked them . . . The first thing that came to my mind is a bear attack; this time of year, the bears are very hungry. On the other hand, maybe it was a mountain lion. I was very curious . . . but when I heard what happened, I couldn't believe it. I was shocked. I ran as fast as I could to Yanyan's village. This cannot be. I saw Yanyan's mom and the look on her face said it all; it was a look of pain, hurt and dismay. I knew then that what I had heard back at my village was true.

As I walk back to my village thinking, I will never see my friend again I ask myself; could I have brought this on Yanyan and her village? Could I have warned them?

When I got back to my village, I asked the elders what they were going to do and I told them that I wanted to go with them. Our chief said he was sorry for my friend and her tribe but there was nothing we could do. I can't believe what I'm hearing. He started to tell me that the Pume' tribe are ruthless lawless, and savage warriors; no one knows when they will attack. They set up traps behind them and ahead of them to kill or maim anyone who tries to follow them. They never travel on any trail and never leave footprints. One thing we know that's true, they can't swim. However, we know very well the damage and destruction they can do.

The chief went on, "Sixteen years ago, they attacked our village. Your father was brutally killed protecting your mother. Then a few months later you were born."

I cry out, "Wait … my mother told me and you did as well, that my father was struck by lightning. I don't understand. Why did you lie to me? Why did my mother lie to me?" I stormed out of there confused, angry and afraid, feelings that I had never had all at once.

As I head to my tepee, I come across Namoo and he says he's sorry about my friend and asks me how I'm feeling? Then he says, "What are we waiting for? Let's go after Yanyan." I ask him to wait, as I have a few things I must discuss with my mother. When I enter my home, mother is sitting next to the fire. Before I can say anything, she says she's sorry but she just couldn't tell me what really happened, it was too painful. Then after a short pause, which seemed like hours, she began to tell me what had taken place.

"It was the day of our wedding. We feasted laughed, sang and danced for hours. It was the happiest day of my life. Then, just when the last flame in our village went out, I heard a loud shriek and a scream. Then, there were only screams. Your father told me to stay inside under the covers. He gave me a tomahawk and told me to keep quiet and if anyone came in, not to move, but use the tomahawk if I needed to. I could see through the opening of our tepee everything that was happening. There were men who were neither from our village nor from any tribe near here, with dark coloring over their bodies, Tomahawk in one hand and sharp objects in the other.

Then I saw your father fight one man after the other. Then out of nowhere, an arrow rang out, then two and three. Then I could not see your father any longer. As I lay still in the darkness of our tent, I could hear my heart pounding, louder than any war drum. I can hear my sweat dripping like the rain in a thunderstorm. As I lay still trying not to breath, I looked around and I was surrounded by the Pume' . . . They destroyed our village, killed anyone who resisted and took anything they wanted. They took away all the unmarried women and ravaged the other ones in front of their husbands and children. They are not men, they are not even animals, for animals do not treat their own like this."

I couldn't take it . . . I told her not to say anymore. I couldn't believe what I had heard from my mother's mouth. I was so angry but so very afraid for my friend Yanyan.

As I sit outside thinking of what my mother just told me, my friend Namoo comes over and says he's ready. I ask him, "Ready for what?" He gives me a funny look, but I know what he's talking about. He's says he's been snooping around and knows a place where we can sneak out the village. Since Yanyan's village was raided last night, our village men and elders will not permit any one out of the village without an escort and no one out at night—Period! So Namoo says, it takes a few minutes for them to come around to our part of the village. We'll just wait until the elder that's patrolling our area to turn his back, and then we will have to sprint to the old pine tree. After a few mental rehearsals, I was ready. I turn and whisper to Namoo and tell him that he does not have to come; it's going to be very dangerous and his family won't approve.

He looked at me and said, "I'm tired of this village; we do the same thing every day, day after day. The only fun we have is when we go out and explore the forest on our own. But even that is getting boring because we can't go as far as we want. Plus, when it starts getting dark, we have to hurry back . . . I'm not worried about how dangerous it's going to be and you know I don't listen to my family anyway.

We look at each other and smile. It's time to make our exit. I'm a little nervous and anxious not knowing how this journey will end. It's now or never. The elder is just a few feet from turning his back towards us ... three ... two ... one ... We make a run for it, running as fast as we can. But just as I reach the old pine tree the elder screams and yells. When I look to find Namoo, he's nowhere around. So I peek from behind the old pine and I see that Namoo is on the ground and the elder is yelling at him. Namoo gets up off the ground and heads to his tepee, receiving a verbal lashing. I totally forgot that Namoo does not run as quickly as I do and he's a little clumsy. Anyway, I'm glad he's not here; he could get hurt.

As I make my way through the forest, I travel the path that the animals of the forest take. It's not the normal path that our people travel. This path is denser and it has thicker brush, but I must travel this way, nonstop until I reach Yanyan. I heard the elders say that the Pume' set traps along any path they take to kill and maim anyone who follows them. They have a day's head start over me, so I must proceed swiftly and quietly. As I walk, I can't help but wonder if I could've stopped the attack on Yanyan's village, by telling someone what I had been seeing for weeks before the attack. They were moving very slowly towards the northeast. Was it my fault?

I walk deeper and deeper into the dark, dense forest. It's getting so dark now that I can only see an inch in front of me; but I keep on. I can hear the crickets; every other step I take they get quiet, then they start again. After almost six hours, I'm at a place in the forest that is not familiar. The trees are different, the plants, even the air seems different; so I must be more aware. I climb atop a tree to rest and to look towards the northeast, for that is the direction the Pume' were heading ... or so I hoped. As I look, I can see them; they are still heading northeast. I wondered how I caught up with them so quickly.

I also try to see if I can locate my village, but I can't; there is no turning back now. As I look back on the animal trail, I notice someone heading in my direction. Is it an elder from my village? Is it a scout from the Pume' tribe? Whoever it is they are still a few miles away and the forest is very dense. What should I do? Should I hide or should I move ahead? Just then, I thought of something ... when I was younger, I used to build traps to catch small animals. I was pretty good at it. I once caught a deer. So I climb down the tree, I take out my knife and start cutting some vines and tying them together. Then I hide behind what we call a sticker bush, because the thorns of this bush stick to you and they are hard to get out. Just as I finish, I can hear him coming towards me. I quickly duck down and stay quiet. He's coming closer and closer. My heart starts pounding, harder and louder. Then I think and wonder ... ok what happens when I trap this person? Do I leave him there do I bind him and take him with me ... I'll figure it out later. The person is just a few feet from the trap and then ... swoosh ... I have him! I stay back to see if the trap is strong enough, but when I take a closer look ... it's Namoo, my friend from my village. I get a huge smile on my face. I can see Namoo is not too happy. "Ha ha ha ha. My friend, how are you?"

"Nice joke, now get me down."

"Before I do, I have a few questions . . . how did you leave our village and did anyone follow you?" He said that the elder that saw him trip and fall when he was leaving the village had no idea he was trying to leave.

"He thought I was just being my clumsy old self. So he had no idea you were gone . . . and as soon as I got the chance, I left. So now, can you please cut me down?

"I have one more question; how did you know in which direction I was headed?"

"Well . . . you did mention something about northeast, so I took a chance. I climbed up a tree a few hours ago and spotted something moving ahead of me in the brush, but not on the path . . . So get me down!"

"Ha ha ha. Ok old friend," I laughed as he hung upside down in my trap. So I cut the vines and he falls to the ground and as soon as he gets up, I tell him that the Pume' are half a day ahead of us. If we don't rest, we will catch up by morning.

As we set out on the animal trail, we spot a young buck on the path. When he sees us, he takes off full speed ahead, then all of a sudden he falls in a ditch full of spikes . . . a Pume' trap intended for us. We don't say a word; we just keep moving forward. Every hundred yards or so, I'd climb up a tree to scout the area ahead. We are getting closer . . . it looks like they've stopped so we must slow down.

Namoo says, "What is the plan?" and I just stare at him . . . "Natayo, you do have a plan, don't you? Please tell me you have a plan.

I tell him "Of course I do; when did you know me not to have a plan?" Actually, I have no idea how I'm going to rescue Yanyan.

We have never been this far away from our village the trees and plants are so different here; nothing is familiar. One thing is certain. I can hear a stream or some type of flowing water not too far away. As we get closer, I climb to the top of a tree. Yes, I can see the full Pume' camp now. It's not as big as I expected, so that is a good thing. I can see the warriors setting traps; I also see that they have a scout looking to see if anyone is following them. He has a bow and arrow, that much is certain. The stream I heard is a river and much bigger than I assumed. I can also see a tribe across the river . . . is it the home of Pume'? If it is then why did they stop?

I climb back down the tree to tell Namoo that we must get closer and rescue Yanyan before they reach their home. I tell him I've seen a tribe across the river and I think it might be their home; but why they seemed to be going around the river and not across with canoes has me perplexed. Then Namoo reminds me that the Pume' are not good swimmers.

We get a little closer and I see all the men near the riverbank. They are covering themselves in mud. I remember when I spoke to my mother she said they had painted bodies. Could it have been mud? Now I know the village across the river is not their home, but the next village they are going to raid. As I look to my left, I see a cage with around 10 young women in it. That is where Yanyan must be. The women look scared, almost frozen. They are not moving nor talking. A few seconds later, I see Yanyan in a corner by herself. I run down and tell Namoo I see her and she is alive . . . scared but alive. I tell him that the Pume' are getting ready to raid the village across the river and that when they leave, we will get Yanyan.

It's getting dark and I'm getting anxious. I also see the Pume' getting ready, so I tell Namoo to get ready. We get a little closer and can hear the Pume' talking clearly; but it is a language unknown to us.

As the Pume' set out, they leave one man behind guarding the camp and the cage where Yanyan is being held. We need to study the movements of the guard. He is walking slowly, badgering the women in the cage, especially Yanyan, but she ignores him and that gets him agitated. When we get closer, I notice another guard on the other side of the camp, who is protecting the trail where the men left. How am I going to get Yanyan? They have bows and arrows, tomahawks and blades. . . I just have my blade for cutting vines and Namoo has nothing but energy.

The guard on the path is not paying attention to the camp or the cage. However, that doesn't mean he is not alert. I decide to try to get

Yanyan's attention by making the sound of her favorite bird, the cardinal. So I start to whistle lightly and it works! I get her attention and she moves towards the sound; but I also get the guard's attention. I stop and he just keeps moving along. I go back to tell Namoo and he has a rabbit in his hands. I tell him that this is no time to be playing with animals; we must get Yanyan out, now! But wait a minute—we can use the rabbit to distract the guards. I knew Namoo was going to come up with something whether he realized it or not.

I tell him when I go back and whistle like a cardinal again, release the rabbit towards the camp. I get closer; it's now or never. I have my blade in hand and I whistle again. Namoo releases the rabbit it gets the guards attention, but my whistle doesn't get Yanyan's. Consequently, as the guard chases the rabbit, I run with my blade and start cutting the vines that are tying the cage. Yanyan sees me and smiles. I get the cage open but the girls don't move . . . only Yanyan comes out. I tell them let's go, but they are too frightened. Then the guard looks in our direction and lets out a high yelp, which gets the other guards' attention. Yanyan and I run as fast as we can towards Namoo. I tell him to run ahead with Yanyan. I will hold off the guards (even though I have no idea how.) I tell him to take the same way we took before, but just faster.

I climb up the tree and just when the first guard is under me, I jump on top of him and we start to wrestle. Now I see why the Pume' left him to guard the cage. He only has one arm and he is much older. I get his tomahawk, which he dropped when I jumped on him, and I hit him over the head with all my might. He hits the ground and is not moving, so I climb to the top of the tree again and hear the other guards loudly calling the other Pume'. I look towards Namoo and Yanyan and they have a nice lead; but the Pume' are extremely fast. I see some of them taking the path where they are setting traps, hoping to reach Namoo and Yanyan. Some are heading in my direction. I look towards the village across the river and see fires lit. I hope the loud screeches have alerted them and they were ready for the Pume'.

I head down the tree ahead of two Pume' warriors. I have a good lead in this thick brush, and they still don't see me. They split up one heads in the opposite direction; the other is on my tail, so I must be quick. I remember the way back so I'm a little quicker than he is. I am at the spot where I caught Namoo in the trap and I quickly reset it and climb up a tree. A few minutes later whoosh!!!! I caught him. He drops his weapons and I kick them to the side. I quickly climb back up the tree and see Namoo and Yanyan stop. No . . . . No . . . No. Why have they stopped? The Pume' are right next to them. They start to climb a tree . . . why are they not going ahead?

Then the Pume' also stop. A Grizzly bear and her two cubs are directly in front of the Pume'. There are three of them there. The Grizzly bear attacks one of the Pume'; the other two run in different directions. One Pume' got so scared that he ended up in his own ditch, the one that killed the buck earlier. In all this commotion, Namoo and Yanyan hurry down the tree and continue to run. I look around and more Pume' appear on the trail heading towards all the commotion. I climb down from the tree and head towards Namoo and Yanyan. Then, they did something else unexpected; they turn left off the animal trail. For sure, they will get lost. So I also head in that direction. It's thick brush, but I can see a clearing of some sort ahead. Then I hear what sounds like beautiful music to my ears. Water, they are heading towards the river. The faster I move towards the water, the safer I feel.

They are still ahead of me and I can see they have reached the edge of a fast moving river. But they have stopped. As I stop and catch my breath, I see one of the Pume' has reached there as well. He is alone and there is no telling how long before the others reach this area. I sprint towards them and I see Namoo and the Pume' warrior about to fight. The Pume has his blade in one hand and Namoo has nothing. I get there just in time to make the Pume' rethink his move.

There are a few logs on the riverbank. I yell to Yanyan to try to move them, jump in and let the current take her downstream. They will not follow in the water. I tell Namoo to do the same; I'll handle this Pume'. He says ok and helps Yanyan onto a log. I start to move around and the Pume' starts swinging his blade around. He catches my shoulder but he gets too close and falls down. I kick dirt in his eyes and he drops his knife. As I go to reach for it, he grabs me and tosses me on my back. He is much stronger than I am and over powers me. Then I have a flashback; everything is the same as in my nightmares. I am wrestling and he gets the upper hand and is over me. He has one hand on my throat, then he takes out his tomahawk then . . . Yanyan hits him over the head with a heavy stone from the river. She just saved my life. I thank her, then, arrows start flying towards us. Many Pume' are coming.

Yanyan and Namoo grab the same log and jump in the river heading downstream. I struggle to get my log in the water with all the arrows heading in my direction. I finally get the log in the water when I feel a sharp pain in my back. Then I grab the log and let the current take me.

I look back the arrows are still flying but they can no longer reach me, the Pume' don't follow. The water around me feels very warm. I look towards Namoo and Yanyan, wave and smile as we ride the current downstream. After a few hours, the trees and plants start to look familiar. My eyes feel really heavy and I struggle to keep them open ... . But we are almost home ...

I try to hang on to the log but I can't hold on any longer, so I let go. I start to go under when someone pulls me out of the water. I'm in and out of consciousness and now I'm really cold and shivering.

I close my eyes; I just can't keep them open.

I'm at the willow tree overlooking the villages. How could this be? Am I dead? The moon is beautiful and bright. The stream that runs through the villages is just as I remembered it. Then I hear some chanting and I open my eyes. I see a man over me with some beads in one hand, and a cup with some liquid in the other hand. I understand him; he is speaking my language. He sounds like he is from my village but I don't recognize him. That is strange because I know everyone in my village. He wants me to drink from the cup in his hand, so I do and it's awful. He insists I finish it.

I pass out again and I'm at my village doing my chores, when I hear a loud screech. It's the Pume' again. They attack, but this time we are ready and we fight back. Our neighboring villages hear the commotion and help. We defeat the Pume'. I open my eyes and see that the man is still there chanting. I try to get up, but he tells me I need to rest. Then I remembered my friends and I ask him where my friends are. He tells me that the current took them down the river towards my village . . . *I have to find my friends.* I try once again to get up and I pass out.

I don't know how long I've been out. The man seems to be putting some leaves on my back. He said I had an arrow lodged in it and that the arrowhead had poison on it. That is no doubt, why I keep going in and out of consciousness.

I ask him about the dreams; they seemed so real. He said that is also part of the poison the Pume' use. I ask him his name and how he knows my language; but he tells me that it is not important.

"What is important is that you get well."

"How long have I been here?" He said three days. I look around and I'm in a cave of some sort. "Where am I?"

He said, "Close to your village; but until you are well you cannot leave. Your village does not have the medicine you need to get that poison out of your bloodstream." I ask him why he is helping me; then my eyes start to shut again.

Meanwhile Yanyan and Namoo are home safely. Yanyan's village is so happy that they are having a celebration. However, our village is not. The village elders are not happy with Namoo.

"Namoo, you and Natayo disobeyed us and because of that Natayo is not here. You put your lives on the line as well as our whole village. What if the Pume' had followed you?"

Namoo speaks and says, "Natayo is like a brother to me, and he cares about his friend Yanyan. Why is that so wrong? Do we not help our family and friends?" The village chief tells Namoo to go to his tepee until they decide what to do.

As Namoo leaves, Natayos' mother calls to him. She says, "I am proud of you and my son." Namoo says he is sorry that Natayo didn't make it. But Natayo's mother replies, "I know my son is alive. I know it; he is coming back to us."

I open my eyes and see the man sitting with his legs crossed and his eyes shut. I notice he has scars on his chest and back. I sit up and watch him. He does not move. I think to myself that this is a strange way to sleep. He opens his eyes and asks me how I feel? I tell him ok and ask him how he can sleep in that position. "That is a weird way to sleep."

"I was not sleeping," he said, "I was looking at all the pictures in my head."

"Pictures of what?" I said.

"Pictures of my past, my present and what I would like in the future." I had never heard anyone say these things before and I was intrigued. I also noticed that he had several different blades and nets.

I asked him about those and he said, "Well, some are for cutting vines; some are for cutting through animal skins. The nets are for fishing and some for trapping animals." I spot a bow and arrow in the cave and ask him if he can teach me how to use them.

"When you get well, I will show you." I tell him my name is Natayo and ask him again for his name; but he ignores me and fixes me some more medicine to drink. He says, "Today you will be able to eat meat." He grabs a blade, the bow and arrows and heads out the cave.

A couple of hours later, he returns with two rabbits. I am out of bed by then. He shows me how to skin a rabbit. "Back home, my mother skins the rabbit," I tell him. He puts several herbs on the rabbit meat and cooks it. I have never tasted meat this good before. He says the forest is full of herbs and spices. After we eat, we go outside the cave and he teaches me how to use the bow and arrow. I pick it up quickly. He is very pleased and I almost get a smile out of him.

"Tomorrow you will hunt for food with what you learned here today." As we head back to the cave, I ask him about the scars he has. "It was long ago, a day I try not to remember."

Back at Yanyan's village there is a celebration for her return. There is plenty of food, dancing and singing. Yanyan is happy to be home but not happy because Natayo has not yet come back. While back in Natayo's village, the elders are very concerned. They have just learned that the Pume' have regrouped and are headed in their direction. Our chief asks to see Namoo. He tells him, "See what you and your friends have started! The Pume' are heading this way again."

Namoo says, "Ok this time we know they are coming, so what are we going to do? Let's prepare to defend ourselves." Our chief sends a scout to the neighboring villages and lets them know the Pume' are on their way and that we are preparing our defense. Yanyan's village took a big hit last time, but they will be at our side. All the neighboring villages also agree. This time we will surprise the Pume'. All the tribes decide to meet at the open plain where we have our gathering each year. Every available man, with whatever tool or weapon he has will be there.

As we walk towards my village, I'm starting to notice familiar surroundings; we are not too far from the open plains. I notice a stream where Yanyan and I played together when we were younger. The man stops and tells me not to move. He is looking around. He says we must get off the trail now.

"What's wrong?"

He said, "The air smells different and I can feel something is not right." So we get off the trail, we stay far enough away to see anything on the trail but we stay hidden in the thick brush. He climbs up a tree and looks, and then he calls me up. When I look on the trail, I notice men heading towards the open plain. He tells me that they are Pume'.

I said, "It can't be! I heard they never go back to the same place they have raided; at least not for a long time."

He said, "Once they raid a village, whatever they take, they feel is theirs. You said you and your friend rescued someone from them, so I am guessing; they want what you took from them back."

"Then that means they are headed back to Yanyan's village. We must hurry and warn them." The man looked at me as if I was crazy. We won't make it there before them; but I didn't care what he said, I was going with or without him.

He said, "Wait a minute, look again . . . look towards the villages." I couldn't believe my eyes. It looks like all the men from the surrounding villages are heading towards the open plains.

I said "Then we must hurry to be at their side." He then had a look on his face that I had not seen on him before. It was a look of determination; almost as if this was something he had to do, or had been waiting to do for a long time. I was puzzled, anxious, and not a bit nervous or scared. "So what's the plan?" I ask.

He says, "Wait; before we do anything, there is something I must tell you."

"I was from your village 16 years ago. I was there when the Pume' attacked. I fought off as many as I could and I must have killed at least ten Pume' warriors before the arrows came. I felt a few then a few more before I passed out. The Pume' gathered all who fought against them and threw them in the river. I wasn't dead and they knew it. They knew the poisons in the arrow would make me drift in and out of consciousness, and they knew I had no more strength. Therefore, they tossed me in the river thinking I would drown. All the other men drowned, but the cold water from the raging water woke me up and gave me enough strength to hold on to some vines. That night I pulled myself from the river and by that time the Pume' were long gone."

I said, "Why didn't you go back to the village?"

"It took me a few days to get my strength back. As I was heading back towards our village, I heard some men who were fishing and talking about everything that had happened: how they treated our women, how they dumped us in the river, and how they destroyed our village. I couldn't go back. I felt I let our village down. I let my wife down." There was silence for a few seconds then he said, "Ok it's time." He said, "We have maybe a day before the Pume' attack. That gives me more than enough time to make more arrows and set some traps before they reach the open plain. I don't think they know the villages are uniting and preparing to fight."

Respectively, I start setting up traps on the edge of the forest as he makes arrows. He hides arrows in different areas in trees, behind bushes and behind and under rocks. He also makes some with the poison that the Pume' used on him. I ask him why the arrows are scattered about. He said, "When the arrows run out in one location, we must run and try not to be seen until we get to the next location; so that they think, we are many. You will be on one side, I will be on the other and we will meet in the middle.

"Ok, then what?"

"Well then we take our tomahawks out and fight like we have never fought before."

As the villagers go towards the open plain, the women and children are by the streams with canoes ready to head down stream should the Pume' get to them. Yanyan wants to fight but her mother tells her she needs to help the women and children. Namoo and the men are positioning themselves close to the open plain; hiding and waiting for the Pume'. They have knives and gardening tools ready to fight.

"But will it be enough? The Pume' have so much experience in combat. I just hope we surprise them enough to make them think about ever attacking our villages again.

As we rest, the man is sitting with his legs crossed and his eyes closed mumbling some words too low for me to hear. I guess he is looking at the pictures in his head again. I just look at the moon and the stars and I wish I were under the willow tree looking at the villages. I wish everything was peaceful like before and I wish I knew this man's name. Well at least I know he's from my village, but who is he? Who is his wife?

A few women in my tribe are about his age and are widows or are not married. Anyway I just hope when this is all over he comes back to the village. He will be an excellent teacher. I've learned so much from him that I want to keep learning.

He stops mumbling and opens his eyes. I ask him what pictures he was looking at. He said that he was looking at what he wanted to happen. I looked a little surprised because how could he see this. I said, "I don't understand."

He said, "I was visualizing all the men from all the villages together fighting and winning. I was seeing us do very well with the bow and arrows. I saw your traps trip up many Pume'."

I asked him if he could teach me to see the pictures in my head. He said it was very easy. I wasn't so sure. He said, "What place do you know better than any other place?"

I said, "That's easy, the place I was thinking about earlier; the ridge overlooking the villages."

He said, "Ok, close your eyes and think about what you see. What is there?"

I said. "The willow tree, I see Yanyan's village. I can see the streams flowing through our villages."

He said, "Ok, now would you like to share this place with anyone?"

"I said sure; one day I would like to bring Yanyan here."

He said, "Do it. Do you remember how Yanyan looks?"

"Of course I do."

"Ok see her there with you. What are you doing?"

"Hey, we are looking at the moon together."

He said, "How does the moon look?"

"It's a full and its really bright."

"How does Yanyan look?"

"She is smiling and holding my hand."

"Ok open your eyes." I was amazed. That was actually easy and fun and it felt nice.

He said. "You can look at pictures in your head anytime you want. Believe and feel as if the pictures are real and they will become true."

*I*t is almost time for the battle to begin. The air is starting to chill. I can hear the owls hooting. I can also hear the crickets. The Pume' are busy setting traps behind them so they don't see the villagers hiding all around. It is very clear that the Pume' will finally get a taste of their own medicine. The man tells me its time.

"Keep a low profile do not let the Pume' see you."

I tell him ok, but before I go across to the other side, I tell him thanks for everything.

He said, "Don't thank me yet; we have a job to do."

"Right," I said! So I crawl to the other side; but before I get there, someone from Yanyan's village notices me. I whisper to him that I have a friend on the other side and tell him our plans. He quietly relays to everyone that I am alive and I am not alone. I can see the villager is more confident now, as he hides with his blade in hand.

The Pume' are at the edge of the forest about to enter the plain. It is pitch black out and they don't know they are surrounded. I place my arrows where I can grab them easily. I'm ready and set to act. I close my eyes and I see us driving the Pume' out forever. I see my friends happy and joyful and my mother smiling at me. I also see the man from the forest reunited with his wife. As I open my eyes, I have a great feeling inside that everything will be the way it should be.

When the Pume' set foot on the open plain, the villagers attack and I start letting arrows fly. They are startled and begin to fight. It is clear they are better fighters, but we have much more to lose. I can see the man on the other side with his arrows ringing out. We go after their men who also have bows and arrows before they can let any arrows loose.

As I get down from my post to try to go to the next, a Pume' sees me and tackles me. I grab my tomahawk and hit him on his head. I get to my next post and begin shooting again. I glance towards the villagers and notice that they are not doing too well. The Pume' are running towards them. I look for the man and he is at his fourth post taking out Pume' warriors one after the other. So I pick up my pace and just let the arrows flood the air. There are many more Pume' than before, but we neutralized them by taking out the men who had bows and arrows. I'm at my third post. The man has now gone through his arrows and is on the ground with a tomahawk in hand and a vicious countenance that I have not seen before.

As I finish my arrows, it is time to get on the ground and fight. The villagers are being slaughtered. The men from Yanyan's village are almost wiped out. The Pume' have twice the men we have and the situation starts to look grim, when all of the sudden I see a tribe heading in our direction with many more men. I can't believe it! It's the tribe that lives near the great water. They came to help, and just in time. I am amazed at their fighting skills. They use their fishing nets and hooks to capture the Pume'. The Pume' try to retreat but that does not go well for them. Some fall in their own traps and some are caught up in mine. The rest drop their weapons and raise their hands as if to say we give up. They are defeated . . . we win!

As I look around, I see that most of the men from Yanyan's tribe are dead and many men from my village as well. I look for Namoo and find him. He has a bruised leg and a knife wound in his back, but other than that, he is fine. I joke and call him "Namoo the Great Warrior." He laughs and calls me the Moon Warrior.

I ask him why, and he said, "Well, I spotted you high in the tree letting arrows fly and the moon was right behind you. Hey, I didn't know you knew how to use a bow and arrow."

I said, "Namoo, I've learned so much these past few days, you will not believe."

We laugh and then Namoo stops and stares at me and says, "You better teach me. Ha ha ha; ok friend?" I look for the man from the forest and see that he is with the rest of the men from my village. They seem very happy to see him; they can't believe it. They call him Natu.

ur village chief said today is a great day. As we gather our wounded and bury the dead, I wonder if the gathering will still be held here every year. If so, it will be strange and have a different meaning to our villages. It will mean that we are all united. I see the man and he seems a little reluctant to go to the village. I speak to him, "Well at least I know your name and our village elders seem to approve of you. You must have been really well liked."

Natu is not saying anything. Usually he has some wise words to say but he says nothing. I say to myself, *maybe all this is too much for him to take in at once.* I say, "You must be excited to see your wife." He is silent;

he doesn't say a word. We continue walking; I can't wait to see my mother and to see Yanyan. We are at the Ridge overlooking the villages. It is even more beautiful than I remembered. As I look towards my village, I can see a lot of commotion going on. They must have already heard of our victory. I know a lot of women and children will be sad; but I know one woman who will be really surprised and that is Natu's wife. I am so happy to be home.

From a distance, I can see my mother and she is full of tears. I run to her and give her a great big hug. She is sobbing uncontrollably. A few tears come out of my eyes and I quickly wipe them away. I don't want anyone to see that the Moon Warrior has a soft side. I notice that someone is standing behind me. I turnaround and it's Natu. I said, "Have you found your wife?" Then I quickly say, "This is my mother." They both stare at each other in shock and amazement. Natu has tears streaming from his eyes. No words are said then they embrace. I'm a little confused.

Then mother said, "This is your father."

No words came out. I didn't know how to react. He sticks out his hand and I grab it. "I knew there was a connection between us," I tell Natu, "but I didn't know what it was."

He said, "I felt it as well."

Then I hear my name being called out. "Natayo! Natayo!" It's Yanyan, I hug her; we hold hands and just smile.

All the small tribes and villages that helped us defeat the Pume' agree to stand united as one great tribe; even the tribe that lives near the great water. This is amazing. Yanyan is home safe, my father is alive and all the tribes are united. Today is a great day.

ACKNOWLEDGEMENTS

I would like to thank and acknowledge Mr. Kenneth Hirst, for the use of the American Indian fonts and symbols used throughout this book.

In addition, I would like to thank Ms. Carol Ann Johnson, for helping me to bring this work to life by editing and designing both the book and the cover.